Susan Steggall's other titles for Frances Lincoln include
Diggers!; On the Road; The Life of a Car; Busy Boats; Red Car, Red Bus and
Following the Tractor. All of her illustrations are intricate collages made
from many different kinds of manufactured and handmade papers.
Susan lives with her family in the New Forest. Find out more about
Susan Steggall's books at www.susansteggall.co.uk

BC
144

15

2000
A.D.

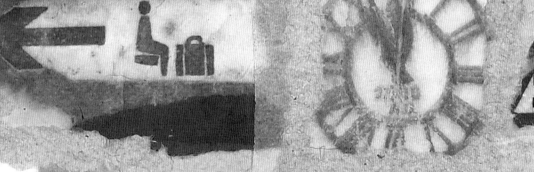

30

840126

For Mollie, Archie and Ed, with very much love

First published in Great Britain in 2008 and in the USA in 2009 by
Frances Lincoln Children's Books, 74-77 White Lion Street, London N1 9PF
www.franceslincoln.com

First paperback published in Great Britain in 2010 and in the USA in 2011
This new edition published in Great Britain and in the USA in 2014

A catalogue record for this book is available from the British Library.

ISBN: 978-1-84780-583-6

The illustrations in this book are collages of torn papers.

Printed in China

1 3 5 7 9 8 6 4 2

RATTLE
AND RAP

Susan Steggall

F

FRANCES LINCOLN
CHILDREN'S BOOKS

All aboard! All aboard!
Bustle and fuss, bustle and fuss,

rumble, rumble, rumble, roll,

rattle and rap, clickety clack.

Tickets please!

Whoooooosh! Whoooooosh!

Swishing and swishing
and swishing and swaying,

hurrying, hurrying, hurtling by,

rocking and rolling and rushing and racing,

Skimming the sky, skimming the sky.

Whistle and whine,

whistle and whine,

jerking and jogging and...

jolting along,

end of the line, end of the line.

BC
144

15

2000
A.D.

30

840126

More **Busy Wheels** books by Susan Steggall from
Frances Lincoln Children's Books

Busy Boats
"Perfect for sharing with a group of children at story time or with a
single child at bedtime." – *Carousel*

On the Road
"The bold collage images of diggers, fire engines, cyclists whizzing by and the little
Mini into which the family has piled, are hugely attractive . . ." – *The Guardian*

Diggers!
"Susan Steggall's super-vivid collage illustrations of bulldozers, trucks and cranes leap
from the pages of . . . her amazing account of what happens in one year on an
urban building site." – *The Independent on Sunday*

The Life of a Car
"A simply splendid introduction to the life of a car. The pictures are bursting
with colour and will encourage children to talk about their
own experiences." – *Books for Keeps*

Red Car, Red Bus
"A joy of a book for its simplicity and vigour . . . Wonderful." – *Love Reading*

Frances Lincoln titles are available from all good bookshops.
You can also buy books and find out more about your favourite titles,
authors and illustrators on our website: www.franceslincoln.com